Published and distributed by

ISLAND HERITAGE
P U B L I S H I N G

94-411 Kō'aki Street, Waipahu, Hawai'i 96797

To order: 1 - 800 - 468 - 2800

Information: (808) 564 - 8800

www.islandheritage.com

ISBN 0-89610-478-8

First Edition, Fifth Printing - 2006

The Tale of Rabbit Island

"An Old Hawaiian Story that I just made up."

by

Patrick Ching

DEDICATION

To my daughter Kawena:

"May you always recognize the beauty that surrounds you."

FOREWORD

The Tale of Rabbit Island is based on daydreams I've collected while surfing, fishing, or driving the coastline of Makapuʻu. This book was written in English but includes some Hawaiian words, some of which are pluralized here in the context of English. It is not intended to represent any traditional Hawaiian legends and was written with respect in my heart for Hawaiian culture and the *ʻāina* (living earth). I hope that you enjoy reading it or having it read to you.

Please remember that Mānana is the true name of the island nicknamed "Rabbit Island", and that Hawaiian place names are sacred; they should be learned and used. Following *The Tale of Rabbit Island* is more information on some of the places and animals mentioned in the story.

Happy Daydreams,
Patrick Ching

It happened long ago, at the place called Makapuʻu, where the cliffs of Oʻahu fall into the sea and the sun climbs out from the darkness to warm the morning sky.

Just off shore, on the tiny island of Mānana, lived a community of seabirds. There were sooty terns, noddies, tropicbirds and shearwaters. Living around the birds was a family of rabbits named the Lāpaki (rabbit) family.

The birds and rabbits got along well because the birds liked to eat fish, not rabbits, and the rabbits liked to eat plants, not birds.

1

One rabbit was especially liked by the birds. They called him "Hapa", which in Hawaiian means "half". The birds thought of him as half rabbit and half bird, and besides, "Hapa" sounds like "Hopper". Hapa loved the birds, too, and often wished he could be one of them.

Every chance he got Hapa would spend time with the birds and help them with their chores. He gathered twigs for the sooty terns and noddies to build their nests. He even played "pick up sticks" with their chicks.

One of Hapa's favorite pastimes was helping the tropicbirds clean their long, red tail feathers. How he wished he could have such beautiful clothes.

When it was time for the shearwaters to dig their nesting burrows, Hapa was always willing to lend a hand (or a foot). He was so good at digging that the shearwaters always called upon him to remove stubborn rocks or dig around difficult roots.

Sometimes when husband and wife sea birds wanted to go flying together, Hapa would eggsit for them.

To thank him, the birds often flew over to O'ahu and brought back some of his favorite greens. The vegetables from nearby Waimānalo town were especially tasty. "The best in the world!" Hapa would say.

Every morning, as sure as the sun would rise, dozens of red-footed booby birds flew past Mānana Island. The boobies nested on Oʻahu at Mōkapu peninsula in Kāneʻohe. They were heading for their favorite fishing grounds many miles out to sea. One of the boobies, named "Ruby", was especially fond of Hapa Rabbit. As she flew by she would always do somersaults and other goofy things to make Hapa laugh.

All day long, Ruby and the other boobies hunted for food. When she spotted a school of fish she'd tuck her wings in and dive into the sea. She could even chase a fish under water!

Ruby was a good hunter and stored her catch in her belly so that she could take it home and feed her hungry chick. At the end of the day, the boobies, with their bellies full, gathered in groups and headed back to land. They traveled in numbers to protect themselves against the thieves that wanted to steal their catch. Hapa watched anxiously as Ruby and the squadrons of booby birds flew toward land. He knew that the booby chicks at Mōkapu were not the only ones waiting for their parents to return...

As sure as the sun sets every day, danger loomed in the skies above Mānana. Just as Ruby and the other boobies flew over on their way home to Mōkapu, dark pirates attacked from above. Hapa yelled to Ruby… "Watch out!"… "'Iwa!" In Hawaiian, *'iwa* means "thief," a very fitting name for the black birds that steal food from other birds.

The sky soon became a war zone as the 'iwa birds
ganged up on the booby birds that got separated from
their squadrons. The 'iwas chased the boobies through the
air at high speeds, harassing them until they dropped their
precious fish. Before it hit the water, the 'iwas swooped down
and snatched the fish in mid-air and then flew off.

Hapa witnessed this ambush day after day. He felt helpless and angry.
"Why are those 'iwas such bullies? Why don't they catch their *own* fish?"
he wondered.

Today, at least, his friend Ruby had avoided the sky pirates. The sun
stretched its rays over the Ko'olau Mountains and the full moon arose to
take its place.

Hapa often spoke to the moon, and this night he asked a special favor.
"Moon," he said, "I feel so helpless. The 'iwas make life miserable for
my friends and all I can do is watch. Do you think the 'iwas and the boobies will ever get along?"

The moon replied, "You should not worry about these things. Every creature has problems in life. But I see the love you have for the birds so I will talk to my good friend, Mother Nature. She has a way of working things out."

The next morning, the sun came up as it always did, and the boobies flew out to sea as they always do. Ruby pulled a triple summersault as she flew over the island. Hapa laughed and waved as he watched the birds fly out to sea.

Hapa was in a great mood today. His good friends were coming to take him cruising. Hapa hopped to the shoreline and waited. In a little while, he heard a voice.

"TAXI FOR HAPA RABBIT! Holoholo Honu at your service!" Hapa turned and was delighted to see his friend Holoholo Honu. In Hawaiian, *holoholo* means "to travel", and *honu* is "green sea turtle."

Hapa hopped into the water and swam out to Honu. Then he climbed onto Honu's back and they were on their way. Hapa was a good swimmer, but it was so much more fun to ride on Honu's back. In the distance, they spotted a cloud of spray. "There's Helena!" Hapa shouted.

Helena the Humpback Whale came to visit Hawaiʻi during the winter months and migrated to her feeding grounds in Alaska during the summer. Whenever Helena returned, the three friends would get together and share stories of the past months.

They played, and laughed, and splashed. Boy, did they splash!
Helena was one of the world's best splashers. Hapa and Honu loved
to ride the waves she made when she jumped in and out of the water.

The three rested for a while and Hapa told them of the trouble with the ʻiwa birds attacking the boobies. "I wish there was something I could do to help," said Hapa. "Me too," said Honu. "Last week I saw an ʻiwa yank a booby's tail so hard that the feathers popped out." Helena added, "Just yesterday, I saw six ʻiwa birds ganging up on one booby. They forced him down into the ocean and didn't let him fly off until he gave them his fish."

"Why do these things happen?" asked Honu.

"It's nature's way." Helena responded.

"But we're a part of nature, too! There's gotta be something we can do," said Hapa.

Just then their conversation was interrupted by cries of panic in the distance.
It was Ruby the Booby and she was flying toward them.

"The 'iwas are coming! The 'iwas are coming!" she screamed. "They're
after my fish!"

Over the horizon, the friends saw the distinctive shapes of four
incoming attackers. With barely enough time to think, a plan was devised.

Ruby hovered in the air above the friends. As the first two ma-
rauders approached, Helena Humpback leaped into the air and landed
back in the water, making the biggest splash of her career. The 'iwas
flew right into a wall of water and came down with a hard splash into
the sea.

20

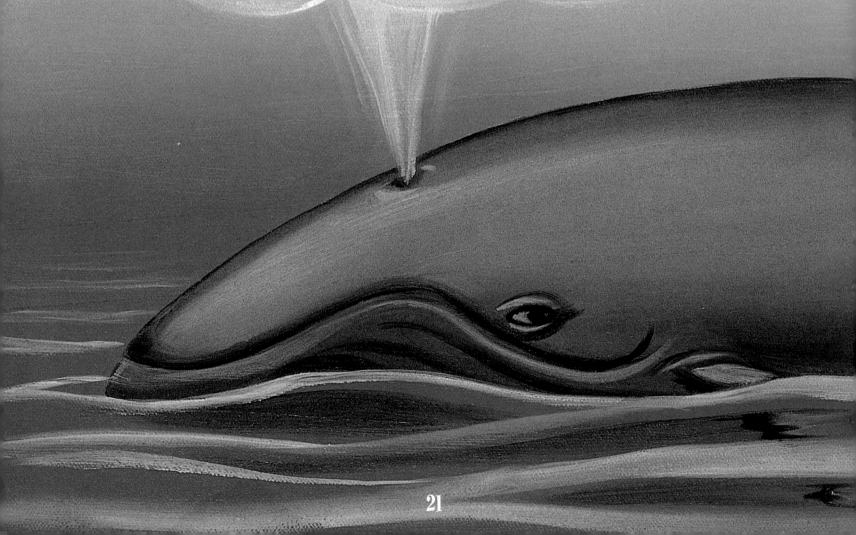

"Two down," announced Hapa, as he searched the sky for the other two 'iwas.

"Bogies coming in low at ten o'clock!" warned Honu. The friends quickly got into position. Ruby looked like an easy target to the fast flying 'iwas, and they zeroed in on her in no time. With one flip of her giant tail, Helena Humpback tossed Hapa and Honu into the air. Then, just as the 'iwas flew over her, she blew a cloud of spray into their eyes, temporarily blinding them. Ruby used Honu's shell like a shield and one 'iwa flew right into it with an explosion of feathers. The last 'iwa flew directly into a well-aimed karate kick delivered by Hapa Rabbit. Then, with a series of splashes, everyone was in the water.

Ruby, Hapa, Honu, and Helena gathered themselves and, feeling proud of their victory, headed back to Mānana.

"Wait," said Hapa, as he glanced back. Instead of shaking themselves off and flying away, the 'iwas were splashing around helplessly,
trying to lift themselves out of the water.

The friends could not bear to see such magnificent birds struggling so pathetically. They turned around, and in a short time, Hapa, Honu, Ruby, and the 'iwas were all sitting together… right on top of Helena's back!

"What's the matter with you folks? Why don't you fly away?" asked Honu.

"It's really hard for us to take off from the water," said the 'iwa leader. "We have such small feet with very little webbing between our toes, so we can't swim well. That's why we steal fish that other birds have caught instead of diving for them ourselves."

For the very first time, the fierce 'iwa birds were not so scary. "Thank you for coming back to help us," one of them said.

"Mother Nature has brought us together for a reason," said Hapa. "Maybe there's a way we can help each other out." The group spent the rest of the day talking, laughing, and thinking up nice things to do for each other.

Because they spent so much time at sea, the boobies knew some of the officers on the Coast Guard ships. The boobies convinced the Coast Guard to build a huge lighthouse at Makapu'u point to guide the 'iwas home after dark. Besides, ships and airplanes could use it too!

To show their appreciation, the 'iwas performed tricks at Sea Life Park, and when the animal trainers rewarded them with fish, the 'iwas in turn took the fish to the boobies. From then on, all the animals respected each other and got along great.

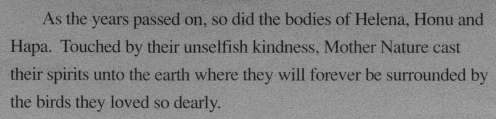

As the years passed on, so did the bodies of Helena, Honu and Hapa. Touched by their unselfish kindness, Mother Nature cast their spirits unto the earth where they will forever be surrounded by the birds they loved so dearly.

Honu became the watchful peninsula of Mōkapu, overlooking Mokumanu (Bird Island) of Kāneʻohe. Helena's hump still surfaces next to Mānana at an island called Kāohikaipu. On some days you can still see her spouting mist.

As for Hapa Rabbit, his spirit lives on in the sand and soil of Mānana, which is today nicknamed "Rabbit Island."

PAU
(that means finished)

I hope you enjoyed The Tale of Rabbit Island.

Now, here are some facts about the places and animals in this book.

Stories are made to be entertaining, but real life is interesting too!

Mānana

Nicknamed "Rabbit Island"

Just off the Makapu'u shoreline is O'ahu's most prominent offshore islet. Its Hawaiian name, Mānana, could mean 'buoyant' or 'floatable', as the island appears to float on the ocean. In the late 1880s, John Cummins, the first owner of Waimānalo Sugar Plantation, raised European rabbits as a hobby. He took his rabbits to Mānana to avoid the chance that they might escape, multiply, and ruin the crops of Waimānalo.

The rabbits quickly multiplied on Mānana and, from then on, the island was nicknamed "Rabbit Island." Oddly enough, the profile of Mānana viewed from Makapu'u, resembles a rabbit's head with its ears back, as it swims toward the lighthouse. The rabbit population rose and fell according to the amount of rainfall the island received, and the last rabbit was sighted there in 1995.

Mānana is a State Bird Sanctuary, and landing on the island is not allowed without scientific study permits.

Kāohikaipu

This small, dark island, often called Black Rock, is located next to Mānana. The Hawaiian name Kāohi-ka-ipu translates to "the container that holds back." This island was likely named for a small bay and cave on the ocean side of the island, which are known to collect floating matter. Kāohikaipu is also a State Seabird Sanctuary.

Mōkapu

This peninsula, originally named Moku-kapu, or "sacred district", resembles a sea turtle when viewed from Makapu'u. Today Mōkapu is occupied by the United States Marine Corps and a thriving colony of red-footed boobies. Just offshore from Mōkapu is the islet called Mokumanu, or "Bird Island."

Makapu'u Lighthouse

Built in 1909, the strongest lighthouse in Hawai'i shines from the cliffs of Makapu'u. Its recognizable beacon has been very important in guiding ships and aircraft (and seabirds, too) safely past the treacherous rocks and offshore islands.

Rabbit - Lāpaki

European settlers probably brought the first rabbits to
Hawai'i in the early 1800s. Rabbits were commonly kept and
raised as a source of food. However, many escaped, multiplied
rapidly, and wreaked havoc on the Hawaiian landscape. Since
then, many wild populations have existed throughout the
islands. Because there were no R's, B's, or T's in the written
Hawaiian language, the Hawaiians changed the word 'rabbit'
to 'lāpaki'.

Green Sea Turtle – Honu

Most of the turtles in Hawai'i are the species known as Honu. Adults may grow to be 400 pounds. Honu was an important food source in old Hawai'i, but severe over hunting in the last century brought their numbers way down. The Honu is now listed as "threatened" under the U.S. Endangered Species Act, and it is illegal to harm or harass them.

Humpback Whale – Koholā

Humpbacks are named for the distinctive fin on their back that looks like a hump. They migrate great distances to their summer feeding grounds off Alaska, where they feed on plankton and shrimp, called "krill." They catch the krill by swallowing large amounts of water and pushing it out past a strainer-like substance called baleen; the baleen located where the teeth would normally be.

In the winter, humpbacks in Alaska migrate back to Hawai'i, where the pregnant females give birth to their young, called "calves." Humpbacks are famous for jumping out of the ocean, or "breaching," causing enormous splashes.

Great Frigatebird - ʻIwa

With a wingspan of over seven feet, the ʻiwa is one of the world's most skilled flyers. Its small feet and large wings make it difficult to swim or take off from the water unless a stiff breeze is passing. The ʻiwa is a good fisher and feeds by flying over the water and dipping its long beak in to get fish. Airborne flying fish are one of its favorite foods. Female ʻiwa have a white breast area, while males are all black with a bright red throat pouch that they inflate during courtship. The Hawaiian word "ʻiwa" means "thief" and refers to the bird's habit of stealing fish from other birds.

Red-Tailed Tropicbirds – Koaʻe ʻula

A pair of long, red, streamer-like tail feathers distinguish the Koaʻe ʻula from other birds. Its body is stark white.

When the birds molted, or shed their feathers, islanders would collect the long red tail feathers to make headdresses, kāhili (markers of royalty), or other kinds of ornaments.

Wedge-Tailed Shearwater – ʻUaʻu Kani

These birds nest in burrows beneath the ground and during the night often make a noise that sounds like a crying baby. Sometimes wayward sailors would hear the morning calls of the shearwaters and not see the birds. This made them think the islands were haunted.

On Mānana Island, rabbits sometimes shared burrows with nesting Shearwaters.

Red-Footed Booby - ʻĀ

There are three species of booby birds that live in Hawaii: masked, brown, and red-footed boobies. They share the same Hawaiian name, " ʻā," which sounds like the calls they make.

Most seabirds live on the northwest Hawaiian islands that lie past Kauaʻi and Niʻihau. There are also red-footed booby colonies at Kilauea Point on Kauaʻi and Mōkapu peninsula on Oʻahu.

This is the first book illustrated by Patrick Ching using a revolutionary oil paint that is non-toxic and stays wet indefinitely. It dries only when the artist wants it to and is set by heat from a heat gun or oven. This paint was invented in Hawai'i by two artists, John Pitre and Thomas Deir, and is what Ching uses for all his illustrations and fine art.